ccev
5

Good Night, Alfie Atkins

Written and illustrated by Gunilla Bergström

Translated by
Elisabeth Kallick Dyssegaard

R&S
BOOKS

Stockholm   New York   London   Adelaide   Toronto

Here is Alfie Atkins,
four years old. He is
sometimes cranky, and
sometimes nice.
Tonight he is cranky:
he doesn't want to go to sleep.
Down in the street the lamps are
lit, and the clock in the kitchen
shows it is almost nine.
But Alfie doesn't want to sleep.
"Daddy, please read
me a story!" he begs.

Here is Daddy. He is mostly nice.
Almost *too* nice. Like tonight: although it's late,
he reads a good, long story about a horse.
Then he gives Alfie a hug and turns off the
light when he leaves. At the door he says,
"Good night, sleep tight." But Alfie doesn't want
to sleep tight. He doesn't want to sleep at all.

Now he remembers: he forgot to brush his teeth!
"Daddy!" calls Alfie. "We forgot to brush my teeth."
Daddy comes. He has brought the toothbrush and
a glass of water. Alfie brushes his teeth. Tonight he
brushes them extra carefully. Every tooth gets clean.

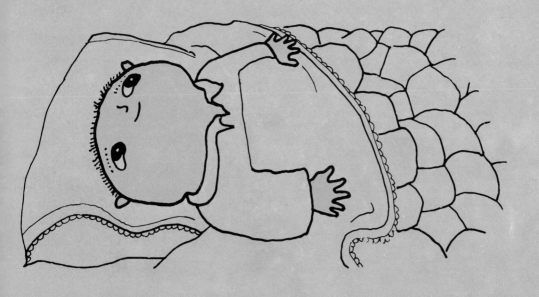

"Now go to sleep," says Daddy, and leaves.
But Alfie doesn't go to sleep.

He is terribly thirsty. He can feel that now.
It's terrible how thirsty he is.
"Daddy!" he calls. "I'm thirsty."
Daddy comes quickly. He is carrying a tray with
a large glass. Alfie drinks.
"Now go to sleep," says Daddy when he leaves.
But Alfie doesn't go to sleep.

Oops! He's accidentally spilled the last
drop of water on the bed. Or did he spill it
on purpose?
"Daddy!" calls Alfie. "I spilled the water. The bed's wet."
Daddy comes.
"Oh no," says Daddy when he sees the wet spots.
He dries the floor with a cloth, and he
changes the sheet on the bed.

"Now go to sleep," says Daddy, and leaves.
But Alfie doesn't go to sleep.

Now he has to pee.
"Daddy!" calls Alfie. "I have to pee!"
Daddy comes. He has brought the potty from
the bathroom.
It takes a while. Finally Alfie pees a few tiny drops.
"Now go to sleep, little Alfie," begs Daddy when he leaves.
But Alfie doesn't go to sleep.

He's thinking about the closet. Maybe there's
a large, fierce lion in there?
"Daddy, come and look!" yells Alfie. "There's a
big lion in the closet."
Daddy comes.
Daddy looks.
Daddy searches . . . No lion.

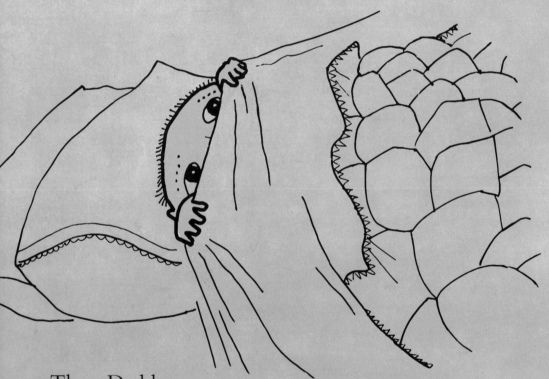

Then Daddy says,
"You don't find lions in closets very often. Good night,
sleep tight, and don't call me anymore because now
I'm quite tired."
But Alfie still doesn't go to sleep.

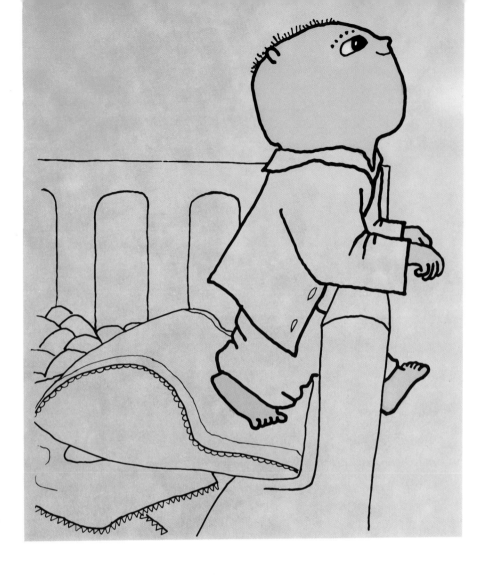

Naturally, he needs his teddy bear.
"Daddy! Teddy bear!" calls Alfie.
And Daddy looks for it. He looks in the kitchen
and in the hall. At last he finds it all the way
under the couch in the living room. But Daddy
doesn't bring Teddy. How strange! What's taking
him so long? Why doesn't he come?

21

Have a look!
Now Daddy has
    read a story,
    gotten the toothbrush,
    brought a drink,
    changed the sheet on the bed,
    cleaned up the water,
    brought the potty,
    looked for a lion,
    found Teddy . . .

. . . and gotten very tired.
So tired that he has fallen
asleep on the floor right after
pulling Teddy out from under
the couch. He is lying there
snoring loudly.

23

Alfie feels like laughing out loud. Daddy looks so funny lying there sleeping. Alfie takes a blanket and tucks it in around Daddy.

"Good night, sleep tight,"
says Alfie, and he goes to
his room. He's thinking that
he won't call for Daddy anymore.
A daddy who is sleeping can't come
running to take care of things. And if no
one comes when you call, you might as well
be quiet.

And NOW Alfie can sleep, too.
Shhh . . . Quiet! It looks as if he's sleeping?
Yes, look! Now he's sleeping.

Good night, Alfie Atkins!